Breathing the Monster
Alive

i

ii

Breathing the Monster Alive

Eric Gansworth

Bright Hill Press

Treadwell, New York
2006

Also by Eric Gansworth

Novels

Mending Skins

Smoke Dancing

Indian Summers

Poetry

Nickel Eclipse: Iroquois Moon

iv

Breathing the Monster Alive

By Eric Gansworth

Bright Hill Press Word & Image Series, No. 1

Cover Art: Eric Gansworth
Book Design: Bertha Rogers
Editor in Chief: Bertha Rogers
Editorial Assistant: Lawrence E. Shaw
Editorial Intern: Meghan Francisco

Library of Congress Cataloging-in-Publication Data

Gansworth, Eric L.
   Breathing the monster alive / Eric Gansworth. -- 1st ed.
     p. cm. -- (Bright Hill Press word & image series ; no. 1)
   ISBN-13: 978-1-892471-40-6 (alk. paper)
   ISBN-10: 1-892471-40-X (alk. paper)
   I. Title.
   PS3557.A5196B74 2006
   813'.54--dc22

                                    2006024900

Breathing the Monster Alive is published by Bright Hill Press, Inc., a not-for-profit, 501(c))(3), literary and educational organization founded in 1992. The organization is registered with the New York State Department of State, Office of Charities Registration. Publication of *Breathing the Monster Alive* is made possible, in part, with public funds from the Literature Program of the New York State Council on the Arts, a State Agency.

Editorial Address
Bright Hill Press, Inc.
94 Church Street, POB 193
Treadwell, NY 13846-0193
Voice / Fax: 607-829-5055
Web Site: www.brighthillpress.org
E-mail: wordthur@stny.rr.com

v

State of the Arts

NYSCA

Acknowledgments

As always, Larry Plant gets first credit for delivering the necessary feedback each different piece needs. For this book, it was his encouragement even as doubt weighed heavy for him. Longstanding trust is its own treasure.

Thank you to Bertha Rogers, whose enthusiasm, suggestions, and interest were instrumental in this book eventually arriving at its final form. Literally, this collection would not have developed without her, remaining instead a series of dark and troubling thoughts.

Thank you to Bob Baxter, who read this book, during its evolution and delivered valuable insights, confirmations and suggestions. Also thanks to Mark Turcotte and Allison Hedge Coke who, even puzzled, still offered encouragement.

Thanks go to Mike Taylor, who rode shotgun through what must have seemed countless sweaty and irrelevant dreams, to Melisa Holden, who delighted in sharing her own secret fears, knowing I would love them just as much, to Charles B. Pierce and his film that still chases me from the woods all these years later, and of course to the people of Fouke, Arkansas, for continuing to harbor one of our mysteries on a lonely stretch of Highway 71 with the casual grace of people who understand this responsibility.

Nyah-wheh forever, to my family, for their continued company on the path of light and shadow, specifically my brother Weet, for keeping the power of the unseen alive for me and my niece Allison, for reflecting that same power, casting shadows into the next generation.

I am additionally thankful to Canisius College for its continued support of my work, specifically President Reverend Vincent M. Cooke, S.J.; Vice-President for Academic Affairs Herbert J. Nelson; Dean of Arts and Sciences Paula M. McNutt; English Department Chair Sandra P. Cookson; and the Joseph S. Lowery Estate for Funding Faculty Fellowship in Creative Writing.

While actual locations, films, and recorded events are part of this work's focus, this is a creative work, and not meant in any sense to be journalistic or entirely factual in its execution. It explicitly engages the distorting nature of memory and reflection, inaccurate and subjective even in the most carefully rendered accounts. Names, places, characters and incidents either are products of my imagination or have been shaped by memory or necessity to suit the narrative.

Contents

viii

For Larry, this walk through light and shadow,
like all the others, on a path where you see
the flowers bloom with me.

x

2

Between Fear and Faith

When I first told my family and friends I was writing a book about Bigfoot, the reactions were varied, some believing I was referring to the fallen Indian leader, others suggesting I was living the dream of every child raised in the 1970s, but all settled into the same general category of one question: Why? The responses then moved into two categories—puzzlement and hostility. One friend from college confessed to her own irrational childhood fear of a promotional item, a large vinyl doll of Mr. Clean that her grandmother kept in a box with other assorted toys. She found this amusing, in retrospect, but couldn't see the feasibility of a book on such a topic. The other, hostile response seemed to grow from the feeling of slight. People wondered, with obvious indignation in some cases, how I could equate the Sasquatch, Bigfoot, and in particular the Fouke Monster (from *The Legend of Boggy Creek,* an obscure low-budget 1970s film about a monster living in the wilderness surrounding the small town of Fouke, Arkansas) with Christ or any other weighty icon from organized religion. My answer to their questions lies ahead. I decided to let them wonder, and if they were curious enough, they could follow me on the path and into the shadows, or stay in the particular light where they have their comfort.

When Ted C. Williams published his first book, *The Reservation,* he considered it nonfiction but was told he should call it fiction. He understood that discussions of The Skeleton and the Little People would raise eyebrows in a book of nonfiction and he conceded, realizing that calling the book a work of fiction allowed him to raise the dead of our community from his memory and let them live again on the page. Ted has recently passed, himself, and his second book will be published posthumously. I can't wait to see what is in store for readers, but I also know he had to continue to make decisions he made the first time: what to tell about reservation culture, and what not to tell. What will people believe? What are they entitled to know? It was not until I decided to take writing seriously, attempting to make a career of it, that I realized these questions even existed. I have been asking myself the same questions through three novels and now, two books of poems. And, still, I don't have answers.

The poems making up the middle section of this book, "Jasper

Applebee Speaks," are attempts to find some of those answers, borrowing a different set of eyes. They are persona poems; the voice, Jasper Applebee, is an invented person, a concrete figure to explore the possibilities of other lives, other secrets, other places where someone has tried to shine a probing beam on a place where the shadows and light take turns equally. He is the resident of Fouke, Arkansas I imagined, and these words are the things I heard him saying as I pictured Charles B. Pierce lighting his lights, calling for the camera, and demanding action on the set of *The Legend of Boggy Creek*. I have made my decisions as someone who documents a relatively closed culture in writing, and I know I have made many purposeful omissions. Doing so causes me to wonder how others have faced this same sort of decision; how many people are walking around with memories of secret things that have colored their lives?

As I was finishing this book, gauging these responses to my description, doubt began to creep in, and I considered, briefly, scrapping it altogether. Three things happened in rapid succession, though, that made me wonder if I had inadvertently picked up on some collective unconscious that meant it was time for Bigfoot to re-emerge in the world psyche, which is not to say this book is going to accomplish that weighty goal, but that it is part of something larger, beyond my comprehension of the ways the world functions.

In January of 2006, for a keynote reading I did at Murray State University's MFA Program, I had decided to preview this material. The audience seemed to respond well, but at a party shortly after the reading, someone mentioned to me that Tony Earley had a short story in the most recent issue of the New Yorker that covered some similar ground. This is of course not what a writer wants to hear upon final preparations of a manuscript, but I dutifully read the story and found that indeed, this figure seemed to be making a comeback, and I was happy to see the ethereal take Earley had on this being.

Though he has no way of knowing this, Earley and I had, at very different times, stayed in the same house during artist residencies at The Seaside Institute in Florida, and I vaguely wondered if some residue of Sasquatch, Bigfoot, the Skunk Ape, the Fouke Monster had somehow permeated both of our imaginations in that house, or perhaps it was merely another manifestation of the fact that we both turned our craft to childhood reflections at times and had in fact a few years before both had work included in an anthology with that focus.

About a week or so later, a friend emailed me a news story saying a group of scientists had loaded cameras and headed into the dense wilds of Malaysia after a village family claimed to have seen a group of similar-sounding creatures on a shoreline, foraging and disappearing into into the dense growth once spotted. It seemed unlikely that Malaysian villagers were watching questionably budgeted American films from the 1970s, so again I was left to wonder over this being. I have not yet heard if these scientists found anything, continue to search, or have just packed up their cameras and flown home to their orderly urban lives.

The last thing that confirmed I should continue in this pursuit came in the unlikely form of a conversation with one of my nieces, Allison. She was initially scandalized when I told her the subject. We had shared much of our early life together, and, after long years have, in adulthood, rediscovered the mysteries of familial connections. Usually, she is supportive of my work, and so her horrified reaction was surprising. She decided then to tell me something she never had before.

Several years ago, when she was first dating her boyfriend, an incident occurred where he perhaps had second thoughts about the future of their relationship. His family was from a different reservation, and they lived in the suburbs beyond the borders of our reservation. She had heard one night, through reservation gossip, that someone had claimed to have seen a Bigfoot in the woods while hunting a few days before. Less than a half hour later, she had a bag packed and promptly drove to the home of her boyfriend's parents, away from the reservation, to a house that was safely flooded with the streetlights of suburban western New York and where there were no acres of densely wooded areas.

Her boyfriend said it was fine that she wanted to stay with his family but he thought she could not be serious in the reason for her departure, asserting that there was no such thing. She informed him that she was not about to risk her safety against a creature that had been clever enough to avoid documentation all this time. She eventually moved back home, and they now, years later, live together in a reservation house nearly surrounded by thickly wooded land. I don't know if they have ever discussed their impasse on the subject of Bigfoot, but somehow I have my doubts. I understand her discomfort and resignation, plain and simple, her fear and faith.

5

6

II. Before the Monster

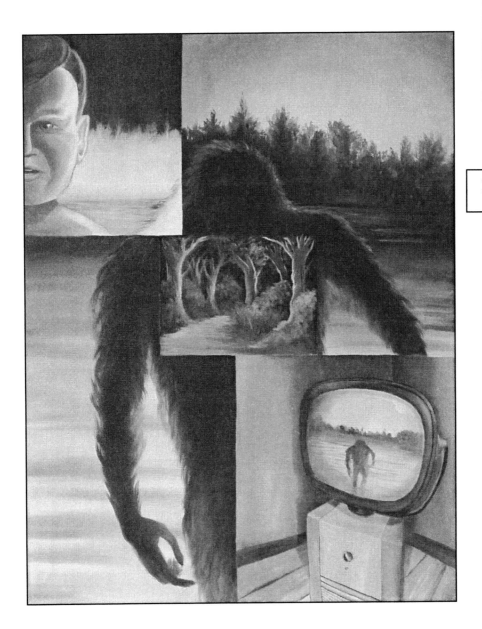

8

Before the Monster

Fear is an intangible, idiosyncratic. What we fear is as unpredictable as what we love. Those emotional responses come from unknowable places somewhere deep inside. For a period when I was five or so, I was deathly afraid of Mary Poppins because I had dreamed once that she was a giant, lumbering up the hill across the road from our house, settling on the front lawn, peeking in our windows to find us.

The dream was inconclusive. I spent the rest of it running from room to room seeking a hiding place though she had expressed no malice other than her inappropriate interest in an ancient reservation house that was not in terrific shape. I had never seen the film *Mary Poppins* and had nothing against Julie Andrews, but her inexplicable guest appearance in my dream filled me with dread for almost a year any time I looked out across the road, expecting to see her enormous body rising above the horizon.

My family thought it was hilarious and often kept me in the living room during the Disney television show on Sunday nights, where brief clips of Mary Poppins flashed across the opening credits. One of my brothers, Weet, delighted in this activity, trapping me, forcing me to face the television. Admittedly, I could have closed my eyes as well, but some part of me was intrigued by the fear I felt when Mary flew across the screen.

A healthy relationship with fear has of course aided in human survival from the start, and I felt that there was a certain attraction in those changes to my perceptions during my adrenaline responses to Mary Poppins. Perhaps this is part of the reason most belief systems involve some sort of fear element. There is always the hope that people will act altruistically in their daily lives, but short of a consistent implementation of such a philosophy, fear seems to be a great motivator within most cultures.

Whether it is the threat of the paddle, the wooden spoon, the hairbrush, or Hell, the greatest wooden spoon of them all, children learn fear early, and at some point in their lives begin to court it for its excitement. I recall doing things I was not supposed to because there was the potential of the wooden spoon. Some children grow and move on to believing in a beneficent higher being and a life of generally charitable acts, attempting to avoid or at least minimize the feelings of dread and panic, but others embrace this more intense side of the world.

I have heard preachers who consistently seem to spread the word about Hell more often than they do the word about Heaven. People whose concerns are more secular in nature, though, also find intrigue in the mysterious and strange, the unpredictably dangerous rather than the staid life of happiness. This attraction manifests itself in organized sports, video games, and other sources of violence or troublesome ideas disguised as cultural activities. Certainly films rank high in their willingness to explore unpleasant ideas from within the world we know and from the world we suspect may exist. I have harbored a consistent interest in fear, from around the time of the Mary Poppins era of my life to the present. Three years after my dream life run-in with the giant domestic, when television commercials first appeared for Charles B. Pierce's low-budget film *The Legend of Boggy Creek*, I felt the same kind of dread I had after that dream and began finding reasons to quickly exit the room when one of those commercials aired.

That same brother who'd held me hostage caught on immediately and promptly improvised knowledge of "The Legend." The film, we could glean from the advertising, concerned a large hairy human-like creature that lived in woods and that had wreaked havoc on the small community existing amid the shadows of those wooded areas. I had already been attracted to movie monsters by this time, the Blob, in particular, and classics like Frankenstein, Dracula, the Wolfman, Dr. Jekyll as Mr. Hyde, sparked by monster models produced under the Aurora brand name. Pierce's film, however, was different from the movies in which those other monsters appeared. At the end of the commercial, superimposed over a freeze frame shot of a man so driven by fear that he burst through a closed wooden door to escape the monster, were the disquieting words: "A True Story."

It was the era just before Bigfoot became a brief national obsession. Now Bigfoot is relegated to the pages of tabloid papers and fringe science conferences, occasionally resurrected when some Asian fisherman stumbles upon a previously undiscovered salt-water fish trapped in his nets, as if our forests were as opaque as deepest ocean. Back in 1973, though, the figure was still on the edges of national awareness, but increasing in exposure thanks to Roger Patterson's famous film of an alleged Bigfoot strolling in the northwest forests. The period between—when it seemed Bigfoot was everywhere—I suspect was in part due to the popularity of Pierce's film. My brother, unaware of the name "Bigfoot," simply reported news to me of the "Boggy Creek Monster."

The back of our reservation house was fifteen feet from the woods—the bush-line, we called it. It was dense, and, while we had paths through the trees, all you had to do was step three feet into the path to disappear from sight to anyone standing on the lawn. The forest plays a significantly menacing role in many children's fables and continues to have echoes in stories for adults, and this connotation strongly exists in film. From Ingmar Bergman's *The Virgin Spring* to Wes Craven's *The Last House on the Left,* the woods are where terrible things happen. Certainly an eight-year-old can be forgiven belief in questionable unseen beings—Santa Claus, the Easter Bunny, and such—but I imagine by seven a lot of children have discovered the ruse anyway. I think I had been done with Santa by then, though flying sleigh sightings on the Christmas Eve television news shows the previous winter had gone a long way in providing empirical evidence through that holiday season.

I was also growing up in a place where the supernatural was accepted as part of the everyday world. The Little People, shadowy figures who guarded and protected children, were ever present. The Skeleton, the Ski-daw-dee, announcing a new death with the movement of winds through its bony body, was a dreaded but real figure in my environment.

My mother was, to a degree, active in the Baptist Church, and we were sent to Friday afternoon Bible school at the church. There we heard stories of the dead rising and other miraculous events, watching the cardboard Old and New Testament figures part water, turn to salt, and perform a whole host of other outrageous activities against beautiful felt backgrounds told to us in unremarkable, journalistic style by older single women in strangely outdated garb—high-waisted floral print dresses with lace collars, as if they had been transported to the reservation from an entirely different era and place: postwar American suburbia. We made no distinctions between the stories these women told and the ones we overheard adults tell one another in the dark, sitting on the hoods of cars over a few beers in someone's driveway. Skeletons and little people, devils and angels—these were the cast members of my unseen world.

I had made distinctions early on, though, between what went on in the movies and what happened in my world. I was intrigued by the Blob and the Wolfman, but never to the point where I believed they would show up on our road. A hairy, menacing figure who lived in the woods, particularly one with the starring role in "A True Story"—that was another matter. There is a large wetlands area in western New York called the Alabama Swamps, for no discernible reason I could find, other than someone with clout must have believed Alabama looked like this place. My brother used my poor sense of geography and convinced me that Alabama and Arkansas were essentially the same place, and thus the "Boggy Creek Monster" was close at hand, likely able to travel through various wooded areas and could be outside our windows as soon as the sun went down, and we would never know. He said the monster liked to reach in through windows, targeting the bed I slept in on the first floor of our house, inches away from two windows we kept open from May until October for cross ventilation.

There were no street lights on the reservation, so when night fell, the dark shadows of the woods crept up and swallowed our hous-es whole, the weak light from our incandescent bulbs making very little impact on the world outside. We played in the dark, my cousins and I, but only in the cleared areas between our two houses, in the faint light offered by the porch lamps. We never went near the woods that bordered the western end of our house. If we played kickball and lost the ball to darkness, the game was over. We waited until morning to retrieve what we had lost. The mysteries in my life were real, and I was given frequent reminders.

An old woman from the reservation, for years suspected of being a shape-shifter, came up to me unexpectedly and held my head in her hands one day while my mother and I were visiting her daughter. The old woman leaned forward and kissed me long on the forehead. Her lips and her hands were warm. She said nothing as she held our faces together, and out of nowhere, my mother decided we had to leave, taking me by the hand and excusing us. As soon as we were out of sight, she dug into her purse, found a napkin, licked it, and began scouring the woman's kiss from my face. She told me to stay away from that woman without being so obvious about it, never offer-ing what it was she was preventing by raising a blister on my forehead, but I understood it was another glimpse into the unseen aspects of the reservation world.

The Legend of Boggy Creek proved to be very popular that summer, and the commercials seemed to air forever. Eventually, I grew acclimated enough to watch them, still filled with dread, all the way through. On our television, a boy my age ran across a dense forest, exactly like the one that encroached on our house. He carried a gun, chasing something, when he came upon the monster, standing in the trees a few yards away. He suddenly fired his gun, but also fell to the ground, tripping. The screen froze, and the dreaded phrase appeared, "A True Story," across the screen. I refused to see the movie but wanted to know what happened to the boy, and I began watching for the commercial, hoping they would advance the story a bit but, of course, they never did. The same boy came to the same mysterious fate that entire summer. I cut out the ads in the newspaper and studied the image of the monster running through a swampy area at sunset, perhaps making its way to the reservation.

The film eventually ran its course, and in time I had forgotten about it, having never seen it beyond the thirty-second clips on television. My interest in horror movies increased as the years went by and horror became my favorite genre, which was well-suited to coming of age in the 1980s, when horror movies reigned at the box office. I sat through some remarkable films and some truly atrocious ones as well, but the quality rarely mattered to me. I was interested in the things that people fear. My first attempt at writing a novel was an awful horror story, concerning a young reservation man's attempt to deal with the tensions of his life, including some of those unseen elements of my childhood environment, as well as the reservation in its more recognizable facets.

Fast forward to the 1990s. Sometime in the last decade, I discovered in the *TV Guide* that *The Legend of Boggy Creek* was playing late at night on a local Canadian station, beaming signals out across the border and into my home. Out of nowhere, my childhood dread arose from stillness, like those Friday afternoon cardboard Biblical characters. It didn't matter to my nervous system that I'd been living in the city of Niagara Falls for more than ten years, where there are very few areas of dense forest, none in fact that are not park areas, and where street lights abound. I wanted to finally see the film, the terror of my childhood. The fact that I was in my thirties didn't ease my discomfort with the idea of watching the film alone late at night, so I set the VCR timer and went to bed, facilitating a safe, daylight viewing. There must have been a late hockey game broadcast that night, for the next morning all that had been transmitted and recorded was the end of the hockey game, in overtime, and a local Canadian news show.

My curiosity awakened, I rented the film on tape a few days

later and slid it in the VCR while the sun hung safely in the sky, casting shadows, but denying the full darkness of night. As can likely be guessed, I did not find the film horrifying, or even suspenseful, for that matter. It was a strange hybrid work, and I could see its influence, however odd, on films and television shows that came after it: *Unsolved Mysteries, The Blair Witch Project,* and *In Search of* . . . came immediately to mind in the ways they paid homage to the film's unusual style.

It was a hodgepodge of documentary footage, exaggeratedly earnest voice-over narration, interviews with people, and re-enactments of alleged encounters with a tall hairy animal that walked upright like a man. Moments in it captured the implied danger of living in rural areas and the dread I often felt as a child watching the sun crawl below the horizon of dense trees bordering our house's western side, but those feelings were incidental, reaction more to the cinematography than to the film's plot and narrative arc.

One brief passage fully awoke the fear of the film in me. When I recognized the scene from the commercials of the boy in peril, it was a subconscious reaction at first. My heart raced and I wanted to shut my eyes and it was only in the unfolding of the scene that I remembered it. I had apparently put that entire series of memories to sleep for more than twenty years. The film went on as inconclusively as the commercial had, though the narrator did state that the boy had gotten away safely.

Two inexplicable folk songs appear abruptly into the middle of the film, an ode to the monster and a plaintive ballad for a Fouke resident who appears as himself in the film. I was at a loss to explain my interest to the friends I'd talked into watching the film. I persuaded some of them to watch many dreadful horror films over the years, but this selection was beyond their credulity and in truth, aside from that moment of remembered fear, I could not believe that this oddly-assembled piece of work had so traumatized me all those years before. We laughed it off, and I took the tape back to the rental store, wondering how many other people had paid a few dollars to have their childhood fears so explicitly dismissed by a decidedly non-scary horror movie.

I thought then that the film had been removed from my psyche by the reality of its execution, but that was not to be. Often, in the middle of the night, where I now sleep on the second floor, feet safely away from open windows, my thoughts turned unexpectedly to the townspeople of Fouke, Arkansas. I wondered what they thought about this document of their lives, if they had regrets about appearing as themselves in this meditation on a being that may or may not exist. They were put in a strange place by the filmmakers. If they said they believed in the monster, and it was proven to be some sort of hoax, they would appear as fools. If their participation led to the capture and potential killing of this undocumented species, they would have been partially responsible for the ending of a mystery in a world where so few mysteries remain.

I had to follow the other path, as well. Perhaps the monster existed, and they knew, relatively speaking, where it could be found, but chose to hide these things from the filmmakers, protecting their own mystery. The filmmakers brought klieg lights and boom mikes and dolly tracks to the small town surrounded by woods and water, hoping to recreate the lives these people had with their monster, asking them to act naturally, but how could they, even if they wanted to?

How would any of us make these serious decisions if faced with that quandary? What would someone do with definitive evidence that the Shroud of Turin is real, or fake, for that matter? Why do people still search for evidence of Noah's Ark? Why am I wasting my time thinking of this small story of rural Arkansas with the same weight these other subjects usually garner among those who are passionate?

A few years ago, I had paintings in an ambitious group show, "In the Shadow of the Eagle," comprised solely of contemporary Haudenosaunee artists. Many artists in the show chose to engage Haudenosaunee iconography in our work, using a contemporary aesthetic. A strong and consistent image was Skywoman, the first woman, who falls, or is pushed, by her jealous husband, from the Skyworld to the ocean-covered earth. The animals already existing on earth—water and sky creatures—facilitate her survival. Among them is a giant turtle that sacrifices its mobility for her safety, growing still and becoming the foundation for this continent, Great Turtle Island.

At the opening reception, I had overheard that western New York's most prominent art critic was touring the show with the curator, Jolene Rickard (Tuscarora). The gist of his questions amounted to asking if Indian people truly believed in this ludicrous story, or if they just paid lip service to it. Jolene's delightful and dead-on accurate response was to ask him if he thought Christians believed the equally doubtful stories documented in the Bible, like a three-day-old corpse rising from the grave. I don't believe, when he reviewed the show, that he mentioned this exchange, but I continue to be reminded of it whenever I encounter people whose faith only allows for the intangibles they need to believe in, discrediting all others.

Sasquatch has, as a substantial part of its origin, a story among indigenous peoples of this continent. As with many Indian religions though, in the face of the zealousness of Christian missionaries, this story was relegated to folklore, quaint and naïve mythology.

Many Indians, as a form of survival form their paradigms in direct opposition to the critic's way of thinking. They pay lip service to Christianity, participate fully in ritual, but would also be the first to scrub the kiss of a shape-shifter from their children's foreheads. I walk city streets—where muggers, drunk drivers, and other dangers could materialize on any corner—with only the mildest discomfort. Dark reservation roads, though, still hold the uncertainty they always have. The reservation is a five-mile by seven-mile stretch of faith, a place where the unseen lives with the seen on into infinity.

III. Jasper Applebee Speaks

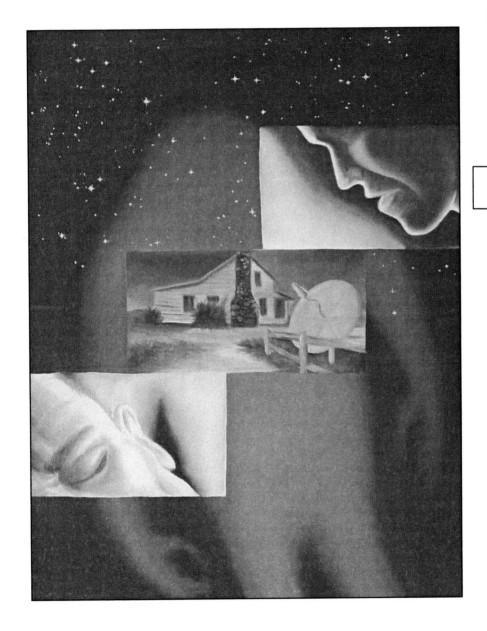

18

This is a True Story

Several people living
in the small town
of Fouke, Arkansas
(population 350)
during the 1970s
appeared as themselves
in the Charles B. Pierce film
The Legend of Boggy Creek,
a pseudo-documentary
concerning a Bigfootlike
creature called "The Fouke Monster"
allegedly living among the creeks
and Sulfur River bottoms
of southwestern Arkansas,
and also worked as grips
on the production crew,
setting up and tearing down
equipment before and after
each shot.

This is Not a True Story

Jasper Applebee Answers His Own Telephone, Probably, Or, Author Intrusion

Finding the listing
was a few key strokes
into the search engine
and there he was, or at least
someone with the same
name, still living
in Arkansas, about fifty
miles up the state's
western border, his connection
a combination of ten
numbers that would open
a door forever if I chose
to press them, let my fingers
do the walking, but what is there
to say, something
like, when you went
to sleep nights, as a young
man, heard that
sound waking you
suddenly, a screaming
coming across the sky
that might have been a wild
cat, or perhaps not, which did you
want most to own,
as your heart raced on that
single mattress in the back bedroom
of your father's house
the knowledge that there were monsters
living in this world or the assurance
that there weren't, knowing that
the answer would influence
who you were when you awakened?

And if I did, what response might come
across the digitized phone line
zero and one in succinct combinations
unlocking that information
I have always dreamed
must be there?

Jasper Applebee Whispers in My Ear Late at Night

It is in my bedroom
where red glowing digits
on my radio spilling
middle of the night music
count out the hours
crawling to the time
when the sun rises
in the eastern sky
forcing me away
from the few
cycles of sleep
I catch these days
that he steps lightly
and I never hear him
until he is right up there
in my face, the scent of Skoal
lingering from the place
where his gums have
receded in adulthood
his hand, as if real
pressing against my chest
holding me in place
until he has said
his peace and he spells
it out for me
P-E-A-C-E
so I will know
what he means.

It is here that he comes
close to my ear choosing
always the left one
ignoring my right

ear, the one wired
into the side of my brain
where the seat of reason lies
instead feeding information
with the steady rhythm
of an old tractor
tilling the firm surface
digging violent furrows
into that side
where the dreams are
seeded and then left
to grow amid whatever
fertilizer might come
along to encourage
them in their trip
to harvest.

It is here that he tells
me his secrets
expecting some
of my own in return
and when I say I have none
to compete with his stories
of encounters with the monster
living beyond the shadows
in a small Arkansas town
a dot disrupting Highway 71
on only the most detailed
of road maps, he says there are
no monsters, only the seen
and unseen, and that I should
know better than that by now.

And it is here that I nod, lie
back, and relax as he lifts
his hand when I do not
resist and then he leans
even closer and opens his mouth
inhaling the air that leaves
my lungs, and forming sounds
words, sentences, histories
he lets it drift
back out into the moonlight
filtering from my blood
to his and returning
always returning to me.

25

Jasper Applebee Before the Monster

Maybe he says, beneath the constellations:
What is there to articulate, really?
It's like those other things
that once you know
them, it seems like you
always had, the time
before growing more
faint until you are left
with a factual accumulation
that you were a boy who ran
trap lines so early
in the morning that you heard
the animals as they awoke
your campfires tearing them
from their dreams, and the way
you preferred their company
to those around
you in the confining spaces
of home and school
so that when you first heard
the howl clearly nothing
like those animals caught
bleeding and dying documenting
your place in the hierarchy
of your snares and spring
loads, you knew
there were things beyond
your meager sense
of dominance over the natural
world, and your view would be forever
changed in the minute it took
for that echo to disappear
across those misty fields
you thought you had known.

Jasper Applebee Shaves for the First Time

Maybe he says, beneath the constellations:
For as long as I can remember
Daddy has done it twice
a day no matter the occasion
sometimes three if circumstances
warranted, pressing the edge
of a playing card from the deck
he keeps on the dining room
table every day of the week but Sunday
against his cheek, sliding it
across the pink and tattered
skin, and if the card catches—reverberates
even a little—he sets the kettle on the stove
pulls his sharpening strap
from behind the bedroom door
and reaches for the straight
razor in his underwear
and sock drawer, then splashes
the boiling water on his face, lathers
us a steaming glimpse of possibilities
before exposing his throat, pressing metal
to flesh and scraping distinction
across his body.

Boy, he says this morning, *it's time,*
rubbing thick soap from brush and mug
onto me, pushing my chin back
until I can barely see
myself in the mirror, *this is*
what separates us from the beasts.
He slides the metal along the right side
of me, nodding at the removal

of hair I had not yet noticed, then
hands the blade to me and says
it is my turn, so I imitate
his strokes on the left side and after
I have completed the ritual and rinsed
my tingling face, he digs back in the drawer
pulls a small vial of sharp alcohol scented
with musk, splashes some into his rough
calluses, slams his open palms onto my face
and finishes me, exclaiming: *You will never feel
more like a man than you do at this moment,*
and I wait for it to pass.

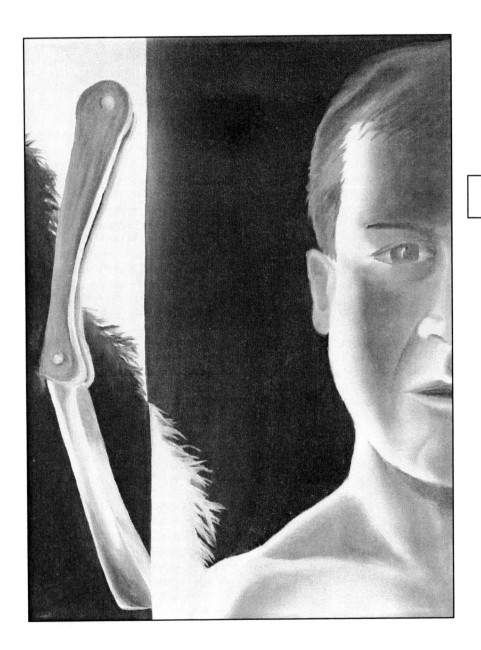

Jasper Applebee Learns a Thing or Two
From the Monster

Maybe he says, beneath the constellations:
The way to survive
is to be elusive
make brief appearances
and depart before anyone
knows what has transpired

say almost nothing as you never
know who might be listening
wanting a piece of you
bending and twisting it to their own
desires and expectations

accept that they will
do these things with
or without you, but know
you can sleep nights
with the truth or your life

steal the occasional chicken
slaughter a random pig
let them know you have
a dangerous and dark
side they should be careful of.

Jasper Applebee Gets a Tutorial on Supply and Demand

Maybe he says, beneath the constellations:
Daddy loved all his children equally until
my brother, or maybe it was me, I can't remember
now, told that there was something
odd in the woods, down near the bottoms
where we'd built our first house.

He had said for years we would
be landowners if it killed
him because we were better than those
others around us, and given the hours
he worked I was sure
he was serious about his goals
so I never argued
when we moved one spring
onto swamp land that flooded
any year we got a little
too much rain, living under tarps
buying wood a few pieces
at a time, or borrowing it
from abandoned homesteads
and praying for drought

so when it came about
that we had bought some troubles
along with the lumber we'd borrowed
he blamed them on me, or my brother
or maybe both, since we had
each heard the cry out there
in the swamps on different occasions
and had the bad sense to tell
about it to different folks in town.

He came home from the general store
and took us both to the creek, made us
pick the switch we wanted to be beaten
with, telling us to look carefully
for a good one so we would remember
there were no monsters
at our bend in the creek
and he whacked us bareback
until we cried like girls
and said the next time someone claimed
they heard strange howling
down by the cat tails, we could deliver
a testimonial, right out in public
that those were just the sounds of two boys
getting their bare behinds reddened
as rewards for tall tales.

He had taught me long before
there were things we were not
supposed to talk about
in front of others, like
certain names for certain
people were only bad
if one of them was in earshot
and otherwise the only appropriate words
and no one needed to know
that Daddy had pawned his mother's
silver years before she'd passed on
instead of it being stolen
during the funeral
as he maintained to all the other
tobacco dippers who sat around
the stove at the store.

He kept that switch I cut close by
in case I ever felt the itch
for honesty again, but on the day
that moviemaker said he was paying
for stories about the Fouke Monster
looking for anyone who would step
forward, my brother up and left
town for good, while Daddy brought me front
and center, said I had an encounter
with a monster, but no matter how much
Pierce shone those lights on me
or swung that microphone
over my head like some voodoo charm
or exposed frame after frame
I kept myself silent, never knowing
who will listen to what you might have
to say, but he paid Daddy for my silent face
just the same, seeing the truth
that I carried secrets
he could not even imagine
waiting for me to slip
waiting to catch something
unseen and unheard.

Jasper Applebee Takes Direction

Maybe he says, beneath the constellations:
Even if you study these scenes
frame by frame the record
will clearly show I knew
how to listen.

I listened when Pierce said
Don't look into the camera,
no matter what; we can't
*afford too many take*s,
was keenly aware
that the man meant it.

Though I never had
to avert my eyes
in the swamps, had never
been instructed by herons
or muskrats to look
away, not make eye contact,
I re-enacted my own
life, swallowed my own
bitter campfire coffee,
take after take, watching
woodsmoke drift and mingle
with early morning steam
rising from the creeks
while a crew of men
and machines recorded
my every move shooting
around shadows harvested
in the rising sun
attempting to invoke

isolation, knowing I would
not piss this fire
out into smoldering, acrid
remains as I had every
time before, and as I'd been
taught by my daddy and granddaddy
before, and I held it
in, pressure building
until someone yelled, *Cut.*

35

Jasper Applebee Gets a Grip

Maybe he says, beneath the constellations:
Pierce tells me that is my official
title, that Grips are important
key members of any movie
production, a must for accurately
recording the world I have inhabited
from birth, but what I do is lay down
fragments of rail track,
along a path he dictates
then try to hide it
among the undergrowth
negotiate the natural world
with these metal beams
crossed one over another
riveted and pinned together
then mount the cart
and camera on these tracks
hang giant lights from tree
branches sturdy enough
to support them, like high
voltage dangerous fruit, wire them
to a gasoline generator
behind a thicket
and when he yells
action, run, gain momentum
hit the camera cart head on,
push it along its predestined path
until he yells cut, when I tear
his world apart, restore mine
and move along redefining
these places as his and mine
waiting for that one word,

wrap so I can commence cocooning
my place, allow it to grow
back to itself, erase the marks
made by his tracks, forget he was
ever here, exposing frame after frame
of a world he cannot control.

Jasper Applebee Cashes His First Check

Maybe he says, beneath the constellations:
The bank teller didn't even ask
me for any identification
knowing I was the boy
in that movie, feeling
glamorous as she sent
my check from Pierce-Ledwell
Productions through her perforator
asking for my Social Security
number then handing over
those strips of presidents
who have tried so hard to leave
a lasting impression, never knowing
that though they might appear
on denominations we trade,
the landmark decisions
they felt they made pass
on in obscurity as we exchange
their portraits for dreams
accumulating them until we can
manifest those elements
of our lives that had been
merely fantasy before fading
in vapor with each morning
in this place where every boy
can grow up to be president
but few want to, knowing the burden
of legend, not so much the living
up to part, but the inability
to do so, that an elusive animal
garners the same status by yelling
its passions as the sun sets
over Arkansas swamps, and who wants
to compete with such a circumstance?

Jasper Applebee Embraces His Fame, Such as It Is

Maybe he says, beneath the constellations:
Well, wouldn't you? Everyone's gotta have
something to believe in, why not me?
A Bigfoot's as good a thing as any.

Who here would not love to say
they had come in direct contact
with mystery? Faith? An intangible
in this world of absolute answers.

Imagine if I had a patch
of hair, or sliver of bone,
a shroud of Fouke, Arkansas

how you would come
to me, wielding carbon-dating
equipment, DNA tests, asking
for the smallest scrap.

Maybe I do.

You'll notice
in the movie, I play myself
paddle my canoe, gut my fish, fry my eggs,
split those yolks in the pan and leave
the shells for someone else
to find and drink deeply and satisfyingly
from my tin coffee cup,
and never once speak of the monster

of the things I've seen.

I carry a gun and a knife almost
all the time
but who wants the responsibility
of killing a dream? Killing "The Legend
of Boggy Creek"? Not me. I let him keep
on going into the Sulfur River bottoms.

I would rather you laugh at me, the redneck
who keeps your secrets and dreams, than hand
them over, like we have everything else,
resigned and tired, gutted and stripped
of every last possibility.

Jasper Applebee Gets a Date

Maybe he says, beneath the constellations:
Yes, I say to her, *that's me,*
before the Landmark
Theatre in Texarkana, ten
miles from the bottoms
where I have grown to this
place, driving a young woman
out of the county, buying her
a burger and an ice cream and only then
pointing to the marquee
where thick black plastic
letters spell out the truth
of my encounters
with the Fouke Monster
we'd all grown up near
and I use my minor celebrity
to gain free entry, grasping
the young woman's hand in mine
concealed by the darkened houselights
inching it closer and closer
to my lap while she traces
the large class ring on my finger
alternately watching it onscreen
where I dip my paddle, pat
the fur of a dead beaver, fry eggs
and then to the place it glints
in her hand gliding
toward indiscretion, stopping
just before its inevitable
destination, saying: *So do you believe*
in things you can't see, or did you
just say that to get in the pictures?

And I, aware of so many
possibilities I have imagined, alone
in the creeks and farmlands, among
animals seen and unseen return
Yes, I believe, and smile, waiting
for the mysteries to unfold
through her spreading fingers
in the dark.

42

Jasper Applebee Watches Himself
On Late Night Television

Maybe he says, beneath the constellations:
Thirty years after the last time I heard that cry
in the woods, the dish grinds to my coordinates
in the backyard as my thumb rests
on CHANNEL UP and I climb through
the numbers waiting for them
to recycle and pass through
hundreds of moments of other people
and, amid their worries, concerns, loves
and losses, there I am
on that bank where I had worn
my own grooves in the mud·
with constant agitation, talking
to a man who these days is probably
nothing but bones arranged
in order below the sediment
recognizable only by the missing
pieces from the time he shot
off a couple of toes stepping
from my canoe, a man who will be
forgotten by everyone, even
ten minutes from now
as this signal transmitted
into thousands of dishes blooming
in thousands of backyards like moonflowers
cuts to commercials offering
the voices of women who will invite
us in digital whispers we can
barely hear to do the impossible
to them for dollars a minute, begging
us to hold off, hold off as they beam
themselves into our living rooms and

fill our needs and in those
moments I almost forget
my own name and the silty world
I left behind amid those disbelieving
stares so many years ago, nearly reach
for the phone, press the combination
of my credit card numbers, and establish
that other connection to another
intangible, like the monster
barely out of reach but there
just the same, if even for only a little
while across this empty space.

44

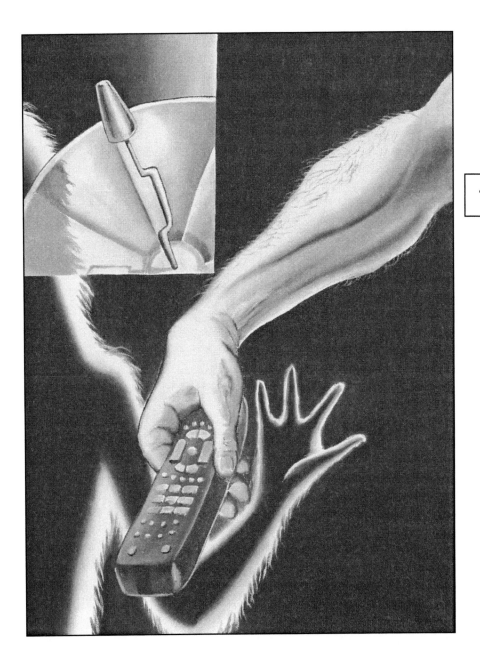

Jasper Applebee Finds Himself in the Liquidation Bin

Maybe he says, beneath the constellations:
There between *The Search for Historic Jesus* and
fourth generation, copyright-free versions of *Night
of the Living Dead*, I see *The Legend
of Boggy Creek*, where I paddle
that canoe of mine straight
out of the box cover, and partially obscured
by my suspended paddle-arm
a buxom woman bursts from her skimpy
outfit, impossibly blond hair shrouding
us as we move, Sisyphian, making dimples
and waves but no progress
on the surface of that murky water
a woman I have never seen before
(I would have remembered had I ever given
this woman a ride) but no one else notices
our lack of movement because all they see
is that perilous shape, looming behind us
and before the moon—the monster, always
the monster, even in silhouette
is more interesting than anything
I might ever do with my life, the monster
who never appears in the movie at all
unlike those days of my youth, recorded
first on film now burning, nitrate eating itself
alive, unable to halt the decomposition
process and here, in this cart at Wal-Mart
as strangers pass by looking for other baubles
to satisfy their voids, I die again
in obscurity, for $2.99, waiting
as invisible particles lose their charge on
the magnetic VHS tape, no longer
positive or negative on their own journey
to ultimately vanish as my bones grow
brittle and memory is made up
more and more of dropouts I must fill in
with anything I can.

Jasper Applebee Enters the Witness Relocation Program

Maybe he says, beneath the constellations:
In Tennessee I age not
as gracefully as I might
like, growing belly hiding
my lower coordinates in
its silvery mat, but here, I coach
for the local high school
football team, roughhouse
with my boys in the locker room
after a winning season, tell them
how proud I am because even though
everyone is a winner, we know that's
not really true unless we're holding
the trophy in our own
hands, catch glimpses of cheerleaders
doing splits out of the corner
of my eye, storing up those
memories for the winter
of my marriage because
my wife wants to go home, back
to Fouke, fishing in the bottoms
listening to the loons
cry back when we would make love
beneath the moon and
stars, naked in grass
our skin gleaming in beams
not caring because we were alone
under that bright glowing disc, not really
alone, but the animals and the monster
cared not one bit for our own
embrace of its ways

though she never had to hear
her name whispered every time
she walked into public
even for a loaf of bread or a six-
pack or two, never had to be
the boy who swore he saw something
few have had the opportunity to
and was fool enough to want
to share, and she reminds
me, smiling, that she heard similar
whispers, and that she had been
willing to be the fool who married
the fool who saw monsters, and by that
very statement, she informs me
she has no idea
what the world is like

when you are privileged
when you are certain that things beyond
science and fact exist, like
the willpower young men have
to keep playing when young women before
them can split their bodies
in two and come back up smiling
before embracing those mysteries
firmly and wanting to keep them
badly enough that they give
themselves up to lives of a dullness
so extraordinary it kills you
in such immeasurably small
ways you wake up one day

to discover you've been
replaced by someone
who never made love
under the moon several times
in one night, not stifling that
cry of pleasure as you both arrive
at the same point together, or

who never saw the monster and lay the gun
on the ground so as to not be tempted
in the slightest, come what may, and

who now in the locker room
after everyone has gone relieves
himself to memories
of young women doing cartwheels
and pyramids and other poses
some perhaps not even anatomically
possible, as they shout their allegiance
to aggressive young men making their way
across a field and life
before returning

to a wife who rejects the past
you share, but who wants it just
the same, though neither of you
can remember the last time
you made love, and neither of you
knows which phase the moon is in
on any given night

and who would go back to that?

Jasper Applebee Follows the Sun Going Down
Beyond the Overpass

Maybe he says, beneath the constellations:
As I came home one summer
for the whirlwind of family
visits before spending quiet
evenings on my daddy's old place
down near the bottoms, listening
to what might be calling me back, there
it stood, unnamed, unnumbered, immovable.

No, not the monster, or at least not
that monster, but across Route 71,
just this side of Boggy Creek,
the only tributary guaranteed
to turn even a half-attentive ear,
the places where I had hunted
rattlers and bullfrogs, there
hunched giant concrete footers, sunk
in sandy earth, growth stripped
away, revealing beach with no ocean
and four new lanes of blacktop.

The progress is slow, changing only slightly,
every time I return to fewer
and fewer family members,
but as supports grow taller
than trees older than my daddy
I can see the Interstate, like everything
else, is moving by us, on its way
to bigger destinations, no on-ramp
or off-ramp, the only cloverleaf
the natural kind that still flourish
in some parts of the county.

This year that road stops suddenly
mid-air, fifty feet above me, no roar
of cars or long-haul trucks, yet, still
an opportunity exists in this place
to catch the sound of that unseen being,
and, at dusk, I drag my daddy's lawn
chair out and sit in the rigid shadow
stretching thinner with every minute
and watch the new growth of weeds
waiting in the silence, knowing this
will pass, given the time.

51

Beneath the Constellations, the Monster Finds Its Voice

I have seen the way
others look through
the tree tops, where images
of some man masquerading
as me, sequential light and shadow
burned onto exposed plastic
in some repetitious spirit
stutter across that expanse
of flatness floating below
the moon as it pulls the ocean
hundreds of miles away and
makes the humans get back
to themselves for a little while
where young upright couples
ignore the ways I yell for some
company of my own, in
their motorized shells sliding
their clothes not off, but down
enough to expose those animal parts
of themselves, determined
their species will not suffer
the absence I feel in the dark
calling this connection love
to soften the reality
of their rhythmic patterns—
survival, this is all about
survival—and that boy, the one
who remains silent no matter
the prodding he gets, from father
from director, from producer,
from bank teller, from potential mate

he is the most dangerous
of them, because he knows
what it takes to survive, that someone
must remember you and speak
about you, transmitting memory
from one brain to another
in repetition and variation
waiting to hear the way the past
has been transformed through echo
and even into the last reel
of my falsified life he keeps
his mouth shut and waits
for me to disappear as the full moon
pares itself monthly to be reborn
again and the sky brightens, as it never
fails to do, diminishing those lights
we strain to see in the dark.

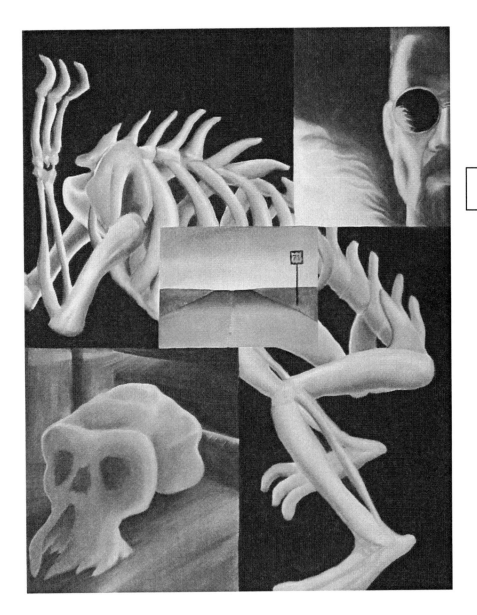

56

After the Monster

The foregoing poems grew out of my preoccupation with *The Legend of Boggy Creek*, certainly, which has kept a light but consistent hold on my imagination all this time, but the poems were jumpstarted in the summer of 2002. After years of not thinking about the monster, there it stood, in the forefront of my consciousness, as I watched the country reveal itself against mile markers and primitive roadside shrines to those who'd been less successful in their journeys. I had decided to visit friends in Texas, leaving western New York one Friday evening in July, after filling the trunk of my car with supplies I'd thought I might need on the road for a few weeks. It was not just my fear of flying that had given me the idea of driving, as I'd made the same trip by plane a month before. There was something else. Invitations for speaking engagements had been coming in from farther and farther away by then, and I had discovered a particular comfort in being alone on the road. It was not the restless "on the road" Kerouac had sought out, visiting the downtrodden before running back to his mother whenever the cash dried up. I had spent enough years in the role of the downtrodden, without any place to run, to ever want to be a tourist in that land again.

Whatever I got from the road was a way of being with myself in the world, removed from all that was familiar to me, at least for the several days it would take each way. I'd found, on the shorter trips I had already made, anywhere from three to nine hours, that new ideas came to me as I drove long distances. I'd gotten a Trip-Tik and map from AAA, plotting my drive around Cleveland, through Columbus, Cincinnati and on down, working my way south and west, and, after having dinner with friends and family, said I'd be back in about a month.

I like to visit locations where films have been shot, and not merely the obvious landmarks, like Times Square, Central Park, Sunset Strip, the winding streets of San Francisco, or even the mid-range obvious, Tom's Restaurant that served as the establishing shot for Seinfeld's diner. I've been to these places too, of course, have even eaten at Tom's, though I resisted the urge to order one of Elaine's "Big Salads." The origins of this habit are unclear. Perhaps having grown up just outside of Niagara Falls has something to do with it, knowing that one of the Wonders of the Natural World and other parts of my home town have appeared in movies over the years, and in each case,

I have scarcely recognized those landmarks when I watched them on the screen, overshadowed as they were, by the likes of Marilyn Monroe and Christopher Reeve in his Superman outfit.

I think the first out-of-town shooting location I'd visited had been the Monroeville Mall, outside of Pittsburgh. Returning from Florida, I cajoled Larry Plant, my traveling companion, to pull off the Interstate exit when I recognized the name of the shopping center where George A. Romero's *Dawn of the Dead* had been filmed. It had been one of my favorite films, and I could not pass up the opportunity to walk where the zombies had shuffled. It was such a strange experience, recognizing staircases, large lighting fixtures, and stores featured in the film that I wondered after the possibilities of other places. I deeply regretted, the following year, not going an hour out of my way to see Devil's Tower. I should have wanted to see it because of its singular place in the landscape of the United States, but, really, it was the Tower's appearance in *Close Encounters of the Third Kind* that caused my regret, and nothing else.

Making my way toward Texas in July of 2002, I realized I would cross over in Texarkana, a town on the border of Texas and Arkansas, and a short drive to Fouke, Arkansas. Fewer than ten miles from Fouke, I drove straight through Texarkana, right on by the much smaller town the first time. I wasn't sure what I would see had I made the minor detour, if I would recognize locations. I had assumed it wouldn't look as it had in 1973, when Charles B. Pierce shot *The Legend of Boggy Creek* around the town and in its surrounding wilderness. A few days later, I was back, with my friend Mike Taylor in the passenger's seat. Somehow, having a passenger legitimized my presence in the town; one of us could presumably be in town visiting a Fouke resident. We drove down Route 71 and pulled into the minimal parking lot of The Monster Mart—a convenience store where, according to articles on Bigfoot hunters, one could hear stories of the Fouke Monster sightings from eager residents.

A crudely-painted image of the Monster adorned the side of the building, and the sign had a curious graphic of the monster happily riding on the back of a wild pig. I recalled that the Razorbacks were some nearby sports team. In the time since Pierce had made his film, the Fouke Monster had become little more than a team mascot, or, less, the sidekick of a team mascot. In retrospect, I should have realized that stories of the monster's permanence in this community were hyperbole, as intangible as the monster itself. The store housed your average assortment of snacks and beverages, tabloid magazines, fishing accessories, and cold remedies. A glass case on one wall held laminated newspaper articles concerning the Fouke Monster, post-cards of someone in a gorilla suit crossing a wooded section of Route 71, and oddly, small tanned pieces of animal fur that had been cut into the rough shape of a man, with tiny holes poked into the head to ap-proximate eyes. We filled my tank, got a cold drink, and headed on to Houston, to catch a rock concert that night. The stop in Fouke had hap-pened along the way to some other place. It was important, for some reason, that the town was never my actual destination.

I returned to Fouke three more times, in the years following. Once, I got lost down a paved road that became a dirt road, ending abruptly at a ranch house's closed gate, and I had to navigate a diffi-cult three-point turn, almost getting stuck in the mud while, I suspected, annoyed residents watched me from behind curtains. Another time, I did my trip laundry in a coin-operated Laundromat just off Highway 71. It was the middle of a Saturday, apparently laundry day for the poorer residents of Fouke. Several bored women stood around, watching their clothes go in circles, ignoring the magazines sitting on a nearby folding table. One man came in, threw clothes and soap into a washer, depos-ited coins, and drove off, firm in his faith that no one would walk away with his wet and cleaner jeans, boxers, socks and T-shirts. He came back a half hour later, moved his clothes to a dryer, dumped in more coins, and left again.

On the bulletin board were announcements of items for sale: firewood, a couple of cars, a used washing machine. A poorly-pho-tocopied sheet of paper warned about LSD being passed to kids as "Mickey Mouse tattoos," the work of some good-hearted parent taking this urban legend to heart. I studied the faces of all who came in, and though some were mildly friendly with each other, almost none re-turned my look. They knew I was an outsider, and I wondered if they were preparing to respond to questions, as they had countless times, about the Fouke Monster. I imagined their answers, shifting glances, odd pauses, hostile denials, or outright laughter at my stupidity. None of their responses would be the one I was looking for, so I went about my business, folded my clothes, and packed everything back into my car, leaving Fouke in my rearview mirror again, having still not talked to anyone beyond saying thank you to the Monster Mart cashier as she took my money and handed me change.

In 2004, I eventually found what I was looking for. I can only assume that the place hadn't existed the last time I had been through, or at least it had not been marked for public awareness. I pulled up to a reasonable looking ranch house on a country road with a large white trailer in its yard, announcing that it was a book store. I walked up to the door and tried it, but it would not turn. After 1200 miles and several attempts over three years, I had found the kind of place I'd been looking for, and the door was locked. I rang the bell on the house, and an elderly man I recognized as one of the residents who had wound up in Pierce's film drew back a curtain. His lunch was on the table, and he said he'd be with me when he was done.

Beyond the neatly cut grass of his expanse of lawn, the woods and tall grasses seemed to wait patiently, ready for the opportunity to reseed this place, reclaim it for the wild. I imagined that Boggy Creek likely lay somewhere not too far beyond sight, moving water and whatever detritus south, eventually to the ocean, maybe washing away any traces of evidence the monster may have left in its everyday acts of survival—breathing, eating, drinking, evacuating. Insects familiar and foreign called to one another, filling the still air with ambient noise I had never noticed while driving, my music too loud for me to fully experience the place.

Eventually, the man came out of the house, accompanied by a woman of the same generation. She unlocked the trailer's door, welcomed me in, and turned on the air conditioner, asking me where I was from, what sort of books I was interested in, the usuals. As soon as she realized the distance I had traveled, she knew why I had come and switched the topic to the Fouke Monster, showing me merchandise in the glass case below the cash register. Much of it consisted of the same kinds of things I could have found, and had, in town: copies of the movie, VHS and DVD, little fridge magnets of the movie poster, shot glasses, T-Shirts, that sort of thing. She said they did a pretty good business at the Bigfoot conventions, traveling around the country to attend them; her husband was a virtual celebrity at the conventions, and he was paid fairly decently when he talked about the Fouke Monster. He had print-on-demand published several volumes of memoir, which I had known about, and I purchased these, along with a T-shirt. After I had made the purchase, the woman excused herself and went back to the house as the man showed me the back room of the trailer, behind a heavy curtain.

The man was a hunter and also apparently a taxidermist, or had interest in that field. He seemed to be proud of the various things he had killed and preserved over the years, bucks, beavers, armadillos, and at one end of the room, a giant snapping turtle. The turtle was the size of an end-table, its skin toughened and thick, and its shell heavily scarred. I remembered that turtles have extraordinary life spans, and I wondered how old this one had been when it had finally run afoul of this man.

In the middle of his tour of preserved animals, he said that he had one more thing on display, and that he didn't usually show this one, but since I had purchased his books and seemed to have a genuine interest, he would make an exception. He took me to another place where there was an outbuilding. He didn't elaborate on what he was going to show me, but claimed that he'd had to chase authorities away from it at one point, which seemed a bit of a stretch. It had been my experience that, when the United States authorities wanted something, they generally got it. Our entire tribe had not been able to prevent those authorities from taking a fifth of the reservation at midcentury be- cause those authorities felt they needed it for a water reservoir, to har- ness the powers of that Natural Wonder, Niagara Falls. Consequently, I had a hard time believing that one elderly man, no matter how good a shot he might be, could prevent federal agents from entering his outbuilding if they really wanted access.

The building was enormous, a two-story high corrugated metal structure, twice as long as the book store trailer. Unlocking and slid- ing the large garage door, he warned me that it probably wasn't going to smell too pleasant, since it was high summer. The odor, riding on a burst of released hot air, hit me immediately, but it was not something I could easily pin down. It seemed like something rancid at a county fairground, like that strange pink sawdust they throw on rotting organic matter to hide the smell of tissue breaking down and chemically trans- forming itself into something else. He flicked on banks of overhead fluorescent lights, and we walked past stored speedboats and engines, an old car that had been haphazardly restored, and many partially- used cans of paint and solvents. It seemed like an incident of future spontaneous combustion, waiting for the flashpoint.

At the very back of the garage, near another, average-sized door, we arrived at what I thought was a workbench covered in a blue tarp. The man told me to hang on a second while he unlocked the closer door. He said I would be thankful for the ventilation in a few min- utes, further explaining that this door he kept locked from the inside so no one would be able to break in. He reached under one of the bungee cords that kept the tarp in place, but then stopped, midlift, to tell me a convoluted story.

He had gotten a call, a few years before, from a couple of hunters, who said they had found something in the woods that they wanted him to examine, given his history. They said if he knew of any way to get some money for what they'd found, they would divide the profits with him, a three-way, even split. He said he had an idea of what they were going to show him, even before they arrived at the clearing. They had dragged what they'd found to the place they'd taken him, by tying a rope to it. He agreed to look at the possibilities and apparently had shown it in public a few times, but had grown concerned over the possible legal issues involved, and had then brought it to its current resting place.

With that, he ripped the tarp away with the flamboyance of a practiced showman. Encased in a large Plexiglas-covered table were the skeletal remains of a large animal that was not readily identifiable to me. The skeleton seemed relatively intact; fragments of straggly hair adhered to a few places, and the tendons seemed to have survived. The man claimed that this was the way the hunters had shown it to him, that the only thing he had done to it was ask some taxidermist friends to preserve it as best they could, given what they had to work with. What he implied was that he was definitely not responsible for what was so obviously wrong with this skeleton—that it was only intact from the neck down.

The one thing that would have most clearly identified the skeleton one way or another was conveniently missing. I wondered, at first, looking over the skeleton, if it were some kind of clever forgery, constructed from animal bones belonging to several different species, but that didn't really seem likely. The animal didn't appear to be a primate, though, I had to confess to myself. Its ribcage was more like a cat's or a horse's.

If I knew vertebrate zoology better, I might know the name for the sort of ribcage the skeleton had, and might have even been able to hazard a guess about the actual species, but what was most evident to me was that it did not seem likely that this skeleton was what the man implied it might be. He of course denied my request to photograph the skeleton, saying it had already caused him too much grief, and he was only showing it to me because I had expressed that genuine interest. He followed this by saying that other people who had taken such an interest had also contributed to the upkeep of the skeleton. I nodded, thanked the man, gathered up my purchases—my contributions, as it were—and got in my car, heading north. Because I lacked that zoology knowledge base, though, I left Fouke, Arkansas with my sense of wonder still intact.

Beginning my long drive back to New York, 1200 miles awaiting me, I could imagine there were possibly rarely-seen primates on this continent who had odd-shaped ribcages. I could also imagine the person who found the proof of this species outside of a small Arkansas town, strange ribcage and all. I could further imagine this person wanting to capitalize on that find, but not enough to destroy all the myth. I could imagine that person taking a shovel, and removing the skeleton's head, burying it, or hiding it on a shelf somewhere, maybe hidden inside of a wall, behind a piece of art, visiting it when he needed reminders that there were things in the world we simply could not explain. I could imagine, even further, that the man dies at some point, and his family finds his secret Fouke Monster skull in some private corner of a basement, the way they might find erotic magazines that could tarnish the man's reputation in such a small town. I could see them tossing the skull away, hiding it neatly among the rest of the man's personal effects, the family allowing it to be taken away to a landfill, where it would disappear among the tons of human trash. I could imagine more.

I could imagine that three men tried to concoct a hoax that nearly caused them a lot of trouble with their community and, in some sense, with an even larger community, but that they did it because they knew of something that people need. They were doing a small segment of their culture's population a tremendous service, giving them something to believe. When all their other beliefs failed them, they could say, "Well, at least we still have the Fouke Monster." I could imagine, finally, that there was something still there, tall, muscular, with long, reddish hair, having perhaps an unusually shaped ribcage, laughing, or at least smiling in the woods, watching the traces of its existence float downstream in the moonlight, while men invented evidence of it from the rotting skeletons of wild cats.

It is a long drive from Fouke, Arkansas to Niagara Falls, New York, where water still flows, proclaiming its status as a Wonder of the World. I live just a few miles from the actual falls, and, on quiet nights, I imagine I can hear its roar, knowing it is probably just the rumble of trucks, crossing manmade bridges over the river. Their drivers have maybe been to the park, to see the Falls up close, or, maybe their drivers have always continued on their trips, safe in the knowledge that the waterfalls exist, cascades crashing down on rocks and suicide skeletons and whatever else is hidden by the constant mists below the falls, waiting to be discovered, waiting for people to say, "I have never seen anything like this before in my life. I cannot believe my own eyes." They will understand, if even for a moment, the desire some people have had, to leap into the falls, hoping to survive or hoping to die, but either way, experiencing a fear and exhilaration unknown to most. They will feel the lure. They will have watched movies where Niagara Falls is part of the setting, and they will suddenly understand that there are some things in the world that film can not capture—something Roger Patterson didn't understand with his questionable Northwest Bigfoot film, something Charles B. Pierce also didn't understand when he opened his camera lenses and turned on his boom mikes in Fouke, Arkansas—and they will want to be a part of that intangible force in the world. I listen in the night, in the dark, and this is what I hear: mystery, the everlasting mystery of the natural world.

About the Author

Eric Gansworth, (Onondaga), was born and raised at the Tuscarora Indian Nation in Western New York. He is a Professor of English and Lowery Writer-in-Residence at Canisius College in Buffalo, New York.

His novels *Indian Summers, Smoke Dancing,* and *Mending Skins;* and collection of poetry, *Nickel Eclipse: Iroquois Moon*, feature paintings as integral parts of their narratives. Fiction, poetry, and creative nonfiction of his has appeared or is forthcoming in the journals *The Boston Review, The Kenyon Review, Blueline, Cold Mountain Review, Shenandoah, The Cream City Review, Slipstream, phati'tude,* UCLA's *American Indian Culture and Research Journal,* and *American Indian Quarterly*, and in numerous anthologies. He has had residencies at The Seaside Institute; The Associated Colleges of the Twin Cities; just buffalo literary center, inc.; as well as at his home institution, Canisius College.

Gansworth is also a visual artist. His work has been shown across New York State, including such venues as the Castellani Museum, the Olean Public Library, the Niagara Arts and Culture Center, the Fanette-Goldman Gallery, Neto Hatinakwe Ohnkwehowe, CEPA, the Niagara County Community College gallery, and Hartwick College; and has been included in journals and art texts. He was also an artist in the Herd About Buffalo Project.

About the Book

The type and layout for *Breathing the Monster Alive* was designed by Bertha Rogers. The typefaces for the text are Adobe InDesign Arial and Berlin Sans Book Type. Eric Gansworth was the artist for the image on the cover; Bertha Rogers was the cover designer. The typeface is Adobe InDesign Berlin Sans and Adobe InDesign Arial. The book was printed on 60-lb. offset, acid-free, recycled paper in the United States of America. This first edition is limited to copies in paper wrappers.

About Bright Hill Press

OUR MISSION: To seek out, study, and collect the work of early and contemporary writers, storytellers, and artists, and to publish, disseminate, and present that work through publications and educational and public programs for the larger community.

OUR HISTORY: Bright Hill Press/Word Thursdays was founded in 1992 by Bertha Rogers, with the assistance of Ernest M. Fishman. A writer, teacher, and visual artist, Ms. Rogers serves as the organization's executive director and editor in chief. Mr. Fishman has served BHP as president and/or chief financial officer since its beginnings. Bright Hill Press is located at Bright Hill Center, 94 Church Street, in the hamlet of Treadwell, in New York's Catskill Mountain Region; program participants are from Delaware, Otsego, Sullivan, Schoharie, Broome, and Chenango counties as well. Programs and services have grown to meet the stated and implied needs of both youth and adult populations in those counties, as well as the needs of the literary community in New York State and beyond. BHP's current administrative focus is on long-range planning, in order to better fulfill its mission and expand its programs.

OUR ARTISTIC PHILOSOPHY: Bright Hill Press is dedicated to increasing audiences' appreciation of the writing arts and oral traditions that comprise American literature, and to encouraging and furthering the tradition of oral poetry and writing in the Catskills. Writers and artists who participate in BHP's programs are selected for their artistic excellence, their ability and willingness to work within a community setting, and the diversity of their backgrounds, genres, and styles. BHP understand that recognition of the need for a literary community and a commitment to lifelong learning are critical aspects of audience development; the organization's programs for children and adults engender the spirit, craft, and imagination that make this possible.

OUR PROGRAMS are offered to people of all ages. Current program offerings include:

•**Word Thursdays,** a reading series begun in 1992 and presenting open readings followed by readings and discussion by featured authors;

•**Bright Hill Books**, publishing anthologies as well as chapbooks and poetry collections by individual authors since 1994;

•**Bright Hill Library & Internet Wing,** since 2004, a facility with more than 6,000 titles of prose and poetry, art, reference, nature, and children's books for the immediate and larger community;

•**New York State's Literary Web Site, nyslittree.org** (since 1999), and the New York State Literary Map (in print and online), developed and administered by BHP, in partnership with the New York State Council on the Arts;

•**Word Thursdays Share the Words HS Poetry Mentoring Program and Competition**, affording young poets a chance to write and present their own poetry in a public competition since 1996;

•**Word Thursdays Literary Workshops for Kids & Adults**, offering, since 1994, innovative programs that celebrate and incorporate the elegant use of words with other disciplines;

•**Word & Image Gallery**, dedicated, since 2002, to presenting works by regional and national artists that integrate words and images;

•**Patterns, BHC's New Literary Garden/Par**k for the whole community, landscaped and creative by Catskill Outdoor Educational Corps, a program of Americorps at SUNY Delhi;

•**BHC Internship Program** for College and HS Students, offering, since 1994, students an opportunity to learn the business of literature;

•**Radio by Writers,** a regional radio series begun in 1993 and featuring poets and writers and broadcast on Delaware and Sullivan County stations.

GOVERNANCE: Bright Hill Press/Word Thursdays is an independent 501 (c) (3), not-for-profit corporation governed by a board of directors representing the community the organization series, and an advisory board from the larger community.

Other Bright Hill Press Books

Bright Hill Press Word & Image Publications

Emmet Till & Other Graphic Tales (forthcoming, 2006) $16
Per Frykdahl

Bright Hill Book Arts 2006 (forthcoming) $16
Edited by Bertha Rogers

Bright Hill Book Arts 2005 $16
Edited by Bertha Rogers with Edward Hutchins

Bright Hill Book Arts 2004 $12
Edited by Bertha Rogers

Bright Hill Book Arts 2004 $12
Edited by Bertha Rogers

Bright Hill Book Arts 2003 $10
Edited by Bertha Rogers

Bright Hill Press Poetry Award Series

The Artist As Alice: From A Photographer's Life,
Darcy Cummings, 2006, $14
2004 Poetry Book Award - Chosen by Carolyne Wright

The Aerialist, Victoria Hallerman, 2005, $12
2003 Poetry Book Award - Chosen by Martin Mitchell

Strange Gravity, 2004, Lisa Rhoades, $12
2002 Poetry Book Award - Chosen by Elaine Terranova

The Singer's Temple, 2003, Barbara Hurd $12
2001 Poetry Book Award - Chosen by Richard Frost

Heart, with Piano Wire, 2002, Richard Deutch $12
2000 Poetry Book Award - Chosen by Maurice Kenny

Bright Hill Press Poetry Award Series (cont.)

My Father & Miro & Other Poems, 2001, Claudia M. Reder $12
1999 Poetry Book Award - Chosen by Colette Inez

Traveling Through Glass, 2000, Beth Copeland Vargo $12
1998 Poetry Book Award - Chosen by Karen Swenson

To Fit Your Heart into the Body, 1999, Judith Neeld $12
1997 Poetry Book Award - Chosen by Richard Foerster

Blue Wolves, 1998, Regina O'Melveny $12
1996 Poetry Book Award - Chosen by Michael Waters

My Own Hundred Doors, 1996, Pam Bernard
1995 Poetry Book Award - Chosen by Carol Frost

Bright Hill Press Poetry Series

Flares and Fathoms, 2005, Margot Farrington, $12

Every Infant's Blood: New & Collected Poems, 2004,
Graham Duncan, $14.95

Bright Hill Press At Hand Chapbook Series
Bright Hill Press Anthologies

More information on Bright Hill Press Books is available at
brighthillpress.org.

Ordering Bright Hill Press Books

BOOKSTORES: Bright Hill Press books are distributed to the trade by Small Press Distribution, 1814 San Pablo Ave., Berkeley, CA 94702-1624; Baker & Taylor, 44 Kirby Ave., POB 734, Somerville, NJ 08876-0734; and North Country Books (regional titles), 311 Turner St., POB 217, Utica, NY 13501-1727. Our books may also be found at BarnesandNoble.com and Amazon.com.

INDIVIDUALS: If your local bookstores do not stock Bright Hill Press books, please ask them to special order, or write to us at Bright Hill Press, POB 193, Treadwell, NY 13846-0193 or to our e-mail address: wordthur@stny.rr.com, or by telephone at 607-829-5055. Further information may be found on our web site: www.brighthillpress.org.

Order Form (may be duplicated)

70

Title_____ Quantity_____Price_____

Title _____ Quantity_____Price_____

Shipping & Handling_____SubTotal_____Sales Tax_____

(New York State Residents, and where Applicable. Note: We cannot process orders without payment of applicable sales tax. Orders of 3 or more, subtract 20% from total before sales tax.)

Member discount (Subtract 10% from total, before sales tax)_____

Ship to_____Address_____

City_____State_____Zip Code_____

CHECK OR MONEY ORDER: AMT. ENCL. $_____

(total includes price of book(s), plus shipping & applicable taxes)

MasterCard____VISA___ Card Account Number_____

Card Expiration Date_____

Customer Signature_____

Customer Tele. #_____E-mail_____

Card-issuing Bank Name_____